WHEELS & HOGS

Connelly's Horde

Novella

By

D.M. Earl

Marguret,
Thought you
would like Book 1
too!

D.M. Earl

For any questions or comments please email the author at dmearl14@gmail.com

This book is a work of fiction. All characters, events and places portrayed in this book are products of the author's imagination and are either fictitious or are used fictitiously. Any similarity to real persons, living or deceased is purely coincidental and not intentional.

This book contains sexual encounters and graphic language that some readers may find objectionable. It contains graphic material that is not suitable for anyone under the age of 18.

Romantic Erotic Mature Audience.

Acknowledgements

I would like to start by thanking a new friend whose friendship and assistance has been phenomenal and unexpected. *Author A.C. Bextor*, whose books I love, not only read an email by a fan, but continually assisted that fan with her dream. Knowing someone can have so much kindness in their heart is refreshing. *Carrie*, no words can ever express my gratitude. You have set an example of how someone should go through life always pushing it forward. You showed me that someone who has accomplished their dreams can also be a true human being and help someone who is just starting to realize their dreams. So, I will start with thank you. My wish is to someday meet you in person and sincerely show you how grateful I am, but until then, know how much you have touched my life and guided me in the new worlds of being an author and self-publishing.

To my friends *Jody and Patti*, my heartfelt thanks for not only not laughing, but for also taking an interest in my first attempt at writing a story. Each of you in your own way has helped me grow and believe in myself with this project.

Jody I appreciate you taking the time to read this Novella, give your input and just generally being a part of my support team. I appreciate you listening to me rant and rave constantly regarding my writing ideas.

Patti, girlfriend your love for reading is almost as crazy as mine. For you to tell me you loved the story brought tears to my eyes. You went through this Novella and found some of my errors, corrected, plus gave me some ideas within the characters to make them truly feel real. Knowing you are willing to help me with whatever I need in this new journey in my life fills me with such a wonderful feeling. Thank you my friend for always being there for me and more importantly for accepting me for me.

Chris thank you for taking the time to Beta read this Novella. Your honesty regarding the direction of the series inspired me to believe in the story more than I already did. Your eye for sentence structure, punctuation, and all around grammar made me go through this book time and time again to make sure that it was the best it could be. You said it regarding how readers hate grammar issues. I appreciate you giving it time straight.

Sam, wow is all I can say. At first after you Beta read this Novella I was shocked. Your blunt, honest, and direct review really made me think about the path I was taking. I was warned that you were going to give it to me straight and you did. After I reread your review, I knew you were right. That is why I started rewriting a good portion of the Novella, but it is now better than ever thanks to you. I am forever in your debt, because I needed exactly what you gave me. You explained to me that from a reader's standpoint, grammar issues can sabotage a great storyline. I appreciate your directness. Thank you.

No words can express my deepest appreciation to all of the Beta Readers for their time and dedication. Thank you for being brutally honest, because now, I can honestly say this Novella is the best it possibly can be. Thank you.

Chelsea Kruse, Editor, I appreciate you taking the first edition and going through reviewing, editing, adjusting, and making this story that much better shows me that there are good people out there. My appreciation for your assistance and talents can't be explained on paper.

Mary-Nancy Smith/Eagle Eye Editing I can't thank you enough for doing the second & final editing of my first book, including formatting for uploading. Your patience with a new Indie Author who questions everything no matter how small your changes were. Even though, as you stated from the story, I am a diamond in the rough you never faltered with my constant inquisitive ways. You always had the best interest of where I wanted to go with this series and realized why this Novella was written like it was. Your professionalism, timeliness, and just your wonderful heartfelt explanations have helped me through many long nights in order to finish, edit, and re-write this novella so it will be a finished book readers will want to read. Girl you are tough, but also have a heart of gold.

Melody Simmons EBOOKINDIECOVERS I can't tell you how much your imagination and ability to see my vision when even I couldn't means to me. I truly love this cover as it portrays what was in my head to perfection.

Dedication

This book is dedicated to a man that allows a woman to truly be herself good, bad and ridiculous. He gives encouragement when needed, direction when lost, guidance when asked (or not). Knowing that I have one person in this world that is always there for me, supports me and loves me unconditionally makes me a better person and stronger woman.

Thank you to the love of my life, my husband. No words can express my thanks for giving me the courage to follow my dream by starting this Novella to my Series. This has always been a deep seated dream in my soul to be able to write stories. You always support me in whatever I do and never let me down. You gently give me a push when I need it to continue when I feel like I have nothing left to give. Baby I love you with all my heart!

Thank you for understanding all the time I have been spending in front of my computer, trying to pursue my dream. I am grateful you are in my life and along with our 'pet' kids our home is my favorite place to always be.

Table of Contents

Chapter 1—The Past

As Desmond Connolly watches the woman's mouth go up and down on his cock, his mind takes him back to the past, when another mouth had been on his cock doing the exact same thing. That blowjob had been way more enjoyable of an experience because he had actually liked the woman working on his engorged cock. He remembered those amber eyes that loved to watch him while her mouth had worked wonders on him. Unfortunately, all he had now were those memories.

His mind returns back to the present, just as Katie smiles seductively at him. Her mid-length bleach blonde hair surrounds his cock and feels like feathers on his skin. Each time her head goes up and then down it feels almost like a thousand feathers moving on his ultra-sensitive skin. As she runs her tongue his the bulging vein, just where he likes it, he feels the pressure in his lower spine and his balls start to tingle. He grabs her hair and gently maneuvers her to the tip of his cock, telling her, "Katie, no teeth dammit, just suck it, and suck it hard sweetheart.

You know how I like it."

As he holds her head, she returns to an up and down motion, and he starts to pump up into her warm mouth, all the way to the back of her throat. Due to his size and length, she is starting to fight him like she always does, and the thought always makes him harder. Even after all this time, Katie still struggles with his size. She is now starting to struggle a little more, not hard, but enough, so he lets up on her hair, as she comes up for air. Grabbing her hard nipples, he starts playing with them the way she likes. He can tell this is affecting her as she starts rubbing herself against him, dry humping his leg while moaning deep in her throat, which makes him suck in a breath. Knowing he has her so turned on, he pushes her back down as she takes all of him in, sucking hard on his cock while her cheeks cave in and she swallows him like a vice. The motion of that action drives him to pump hard into her mouth as he is feels himself moving towards his own release. He doesn't want to cum down her throat, so he pulls her up, telling her to get on top of him, and ride him hard.

Katie throws her hair off her face as he reaches down to position his cock at her soaking entrance, only after putting on a condom. He watches her face as she starts to take him slowly into her warm, dripping pussy. He allows her a moment to adjust to his size before he starts to move and she grabs the headboard to get into a better position. Once she starts gyrating her hips, their thoughts are only on reaching their orgasms. Katie is moaning loudly now, calling out his name, while he reaches between them to put two fingers on her clit. She is so excited that not only is her clit swollen, but extended out of its normal hood and moist from her excitement. Katie actually purrs and reaches around to put her hands on his thighs so he has a perfect view of where his cock is entering her wet pussy.

Watching his cock appear and disappear into her has his whole body reacting as his cock gets even harder. He feels the walls of her cunt start to tighten up around him and it tells him that she is close. Connolly grabs her hips and flips her on the bed so that she is now on the bottom, taking back his control. He starts pumping in and out of her as Katie starts screaming his name. "God, yes

Des, FUCK me, baby. Fuck me hard." Des, as always, is happy to comply.

After a couple of minutes, he pulls out of her warm sheath while she lets out a loud scream, "NO!" He says nothing, but moves to the bottom of the bed, grabs Katie's legs, and pulls her down to the edge. Once she is there, he lifts her legs straight up, and holds them tightly together, then he plunges back into her wet pussy. He starts thrusting in and out deeply, finally able to hit that sensitive bundle of nerves inside of Katie. As he pummels in and out, making sure to hit her g-spot each time, she thrashes her head from side to side while grabbing at the bed sheets. Des knows she is hanging on the precipice of her climax. He is so close but, being the man he is, he always takes care of his partner first. Watching her lose all control and cum all over his rock hard cock brings him that much closer to losing all control himself. He puts his finger in where they are joined to get some of that moisture, then parts her lips and taps quickly on her clit. That pushes her over the edge and he feels her walls clench his dick each time he pushes in, all while she howls her release as she closes her eyes. He can feel her cum, not only around his cock, but leaking out between them running down the crack of her ass and then onto his bed. Her entire body is taut for a second or two before she totally relaxes and once again makes a soft mewling noise deep in her throat. As he watches her, his balls tighten up as she milks his cock and he knows the time has come for him to let his guard down and finally find his own release.

Des grabs her legs and wraps them around his hips while roughly pumping in and out of her. He feels sweat running down his forehead and into his eyes, but keeps the motion going, because he is so close. He feels her starting to twitch around his cock and knows she is going to explode a second time. Keeping up the pace he glances up and sees that she is staring at the connection between them.

"Does that turn you on sweetheart? Watching my cock going in and out of your tight pussy?"

Katie's only response is to put her head down and groan. Des knows he has to get her there because his time is closely approaching. He takes one hand and pulls on her left nipple while his other hand starts rubbing circles on her clit. The overstimulation does the job and quickly pushes Katie into her second orgasm. Des feels her clench around his cock as he drives in. He feels warmth start in his lower spine as his balls contract and he starts to cum into the condom. His entire body tightens up as he shoots his load until he has nothing left. In his mind he whispers, 'God damn, Dee, you bring me to my knees'. He falls on top of Katie, keeping some of his weight off by leaning on one elbow. She is slowly running her hands up and down his back, only stopping to squeeze his ass. She then reaches up, pushes a piece of hair out of his eyes, and wipes the sweat off his forehead.

He leans down and gives her a soft, affectionate kiss on the lips. Katie smiles up at him with a look in her eyes that actually startles him. Des feels uncomfortable under that all too familiar gaze of hers because he knows what that look means. He has always been upfront and very clear about what their 'arrangement' was and definitely about what it wasn't. They weren't what you would call close friends, but they shared a sexual relationship when the need arose.

Neither of them are involved with anyone so this has always worked or so he thought.

He didn't want to ruin the mood, but needed to see where her head was and more importantly, her thoughts. He clears his throat, looks into her eyes, and gently states, "Sweetheart, that was great. As always, you blow my mind and I really needed that tonight. You know I am glad we have this arrangement. Friends with benefits that let us enjoy each other's company while taking the edge off when needed. Just remember what this is and more importantly what this isn't, ok, honey?" Her hands drop from his body, immediately her eyes close. She shudders and softly replies, "Yeah, Des."

After a moment or two of awkward silence, she softly asks, "Why can't we have more? Take it to the next level? We have been doing the friends with benefits thing for how long now? A couple of years, on and off, right?"

Katie's comment makes Des come to an abrupt stop. He now knows, that for him their 'arrangement' is over and that there will be no more sexual encounters with Katie. She's not the woman he'd ever thought of as a candidate for a long term or permanent arrangement for himself. Her reputation precedes her; she is known around town as an easy lay because she enjoys sleeping with a lot of men. Des had no problem with that type of reputation because it had worked to his benefit up until now. But, he realizes at that moment that anything but sex with Katie never entered his thoughts.

Des was not sure he even wanted a permanent relationship. Well, he does want something permanent, but only with the girl with honey brown hair and amber eyes. But, on the other hand, he also sees how all of his friends go through hell with their significant others and wants to avoid the headache of that. He didn't want to hurt Katie's feelings, but he knew he had to be blunt and honest. Never wanting to lead her on, he softly states, "Honey, what we have, we have. I never wanted more and honestly didn't think you did either. But seeing that look in your eyes just now, it's time to say this was a good run we had while it lasted. Tonight can be our last time, our grand finale? No hard feelings honey, ok?"

Katie's hands settle on his chest and roughly push

him away. "Damn you. You can be such a prick at times, Des. I didn't say I wanted this to end, but the possibility to have more maybe someday. Why can't it be more? We do nothing but fuck. Can't we go to dinner or a movie? Maybe you could take me for a ride on your bike. Or, perhaps a ride in your car in the country. Is that all I am to you is a convenient fuck? What I am not good enough for you, because I'm not Dee Dee?"

Holy shit, his head flips back at the mention of 'her' name and he looks Katie in the eyes, "What the fuck, Katie? Where is this coming from?"

She replies with a smug look in her eyes, "You might not know what you say sometimes in your sleep or whom you call out when your dick is inside me, but I do and the name is always the same, Dee. Get off of me Des; you fucking asshole."

Des moves back, to let her up, and she quickly heads to the master bathroom, slamming the door. He just stays seated on the edge of the bed holding the condom in his hand feeling a little confused, and pissed off at this situation he's in. What the fuck just happened? This was not the release he had been looking for tonight. Why was there always drama when dealing with women???? Fuck!!!

Katie walks out of the bathroom dressed and trying to repair her hair into some semblance of order. Des pulls up and zips his jeans, but leaves the button undone. She stops, glares at Des, and then asks, "Is this it? Are we done?"

Des tries to grab her hands in order to pull her to him, but she backs away as he looks her in the eyes and says, "I never meant to hurt you, Katie, I swear. This," as he points to them, "seemed to work for both of us, at least I thought it did."

Katie walks out of the bedroom. She heads down the hall to where her purse and shoes are, grabs both and turns in time for him to see a glistening to her eyes, as she tells him goodbye.

⁇ ⁇ ⁇ ⁇

Sitting in his office later that night, Des looks over some paperwork while trying to get past the blow up he'd had with Katie. He felt like he'd lost control of his life and he hated feeling that way. Des lives for control, always has. He sits back, trying to remember why he'd ever started the arrangement with Katie anyway. His answer was simple ... sex.

She was easy and he wanted, no he needed to fuck, so, he thought it would work out perfectly for them both. It was easy on his part not to get attached, but obviously it hadn't been as easy for Katie. He's never had a problem attracting women, so not wanting any involvement or expectations of a relationship Katie fit the bill.

Des rubs his eyes and knows this little affair is done with her. Kind of sucks because she really enjoyed getting down and dirty with him. She never had any issues when he wanted to go a little dark and kinky in the bedroom, which is why this had lasted so long. She was always available and willing to fuck whenever he wanted. All he had to do was call or text her. But since he hates drama, plus needs to maintain control surrounding his life and relationships he feels relief that after tonight, this is over. Des gets up moves over to his fridge, grabs a beer, and starts to reminisce about his life. Being a loner, except when the mood struck and he needs to get laid, Des has always been fine being single. He values his solitude. He loves to ride his motorcycles, and has always had a gift and love for fixing bikes and cars.

His parents did the best they could for him and his siblings. He grew up in a loving home with the structure of a mom, dad, and siblings. But all that was taken away abruptly when he was just sixteen years old. His parents were killed by a semi-truck driver who was strung out on speed in order to stay awake while on a delivery. His family was instantly torn apart; his parents were now dead and his sisters and brother immediately looked to him for guidance because he was the oldest.

Instantly his life took a turn down a path he hasn't been able to alter since. He'd had to step up and be the man of the house. Even then, he was a just a big kid, but mature and responsible, so everyone seemed to forget he was still just a kid. Des had managed to get a job at old man Leary's automotive shop so he could keep food on the table, all the while trying to keep the family home. He never received any special treatment because of his situation. Des found that he had to work his way from the bottom up. He'd started with grunt work; sweeping floors, and taking orders from everyone in the shop.

As time passed, Mr. Leary realized he had a diamond in the rough as Des started working on cars and rebuilding bikes. He managed to bring new business into the shop and word started to spread.

Des helped guide his two sisters and younger brother through high school and even managed to send the girls to college. His brother joined the Marines. He really never had a life of his own until they were grown and out of the house on their own. All of his efforts went into being a substitute parent for the three of them. He was both mom and dad to his siblings, helping with school work and guiding them into adulthood.

As his reputation, continued to grow due to his skills with cars and bikes, which helped both Des and Mr. Leary grow the business. It brought some famous people and MC's who would put in orders for his work which also helped Des build some strong and lasting relationships with some 1% bikers and motorcycle clubs who to this day call him brother. Des even went as far as to be considered an honorary Nomad in some of the bikers' eyes. He could take care of himself and when on his bike, he was always one with his machine. He had proven himself to the members of the clubs he called 'friends'.

When old man Leary decided to retire, he approached Des and asked if he had an interest in buying the business. Because it was all Des knew, he'd said yes. Mr. Leary worked with him so no loan had been needed. Once it was all said and done, Des changed the name to Connolly's Wheels & Hogs.

Now in his late thirties, he owns the business outright. And with all of his and the shop's hard work, they have made a name for Connolly's Wheels & Hogs. With the help of his crew, they specialize in autos and bikes. Des had some old school mechanics that worked on the older models including restoration. Then he had his young guys who were certified to work on the new computerized engines and cars. This was relatively new to the shop and it was taking Des time to get all the equipment necessary to work on the expensive computers.

The motorcycles that came out of his shop were usually one of a kind. His guys made people's dreams come true, be it a Harley or a custom Chopper; the finished product was something that usually took everyone's breath away. Works of art. Connolly's Wheels & Hogs is known throughout Des's small town in Indiana and even some of the larger cities and states that surround them. Being careful about whom he's hired over the years has proven to be smart and effective. In all honesty, it has turned out that Des has hired people just like him. Survivors, who generally don't have any family to speak of. He has a shop of orphans and misfits who have become his extended family, outside of his sisters and brother.

Des gets up, to take a break from his reminiscing, and grabs another beer, and walks outside to his deck sits in a lounger thinking about his crew at the shop. Des knows he needs to speak to all of them. With his upcoming plans for one of them, he will need all of their assistance.

The only way he can pull off such a huge project is if they are all on board and on the same page. Bringing the bottle of beer to his lips again, he hears the front doorbell, and mutters to himself, "Who the hell is here now?"

Chapter 2—The Present

Going to his front door, he looks through the upper glass and is shocked at who is looking back at him. Completely stunned, he opens the door wide and looks into her eyes, "Dee Dee". "What's up, sugar? Everything ok?"

She quickly looks him up and down, and then motions to the papers in her hands.

"No, Des. Not exactly. You left these at the shop. They need to be signed by you before I can process any of the work. So, I thought since I had the time I would drop them off."

Still in shock, he raises an eyebrow and asks, "You had time to come all the way out here to drop papers off? Really? Where are the kids Dee? Oh shit, come in and sit down. We don't need to have this conversation through the front door."

As she follows him into the house, Dee checks him out. From his thick thighs, to his tight ass, and up his muscular back, her eyes make a hot trail. She finally reaches his incredibly broad shoulders and his, overdue to be cut, jet black hair. Watching his ass cheeks flex under his well-worn jeans, makes Dee wish she could just reach out and grab one of his sculpted ass cheeks in her hands. Damn he is a fine male specimen. Dee breathes in softly so he doesn't know how he is affecting her. Des always has, ever since they were kids.

He turns intending to ask if she wants a beer but smiles as he realizes that she is ogling her way up his back from his ass to the bulging shoulder muscles under his tight t-shirt.

"Sugar, like what ya see?"

Dee blushes and he lets out a laugh.

"Do you want a beer?" Des asks.

"Sure, I'll have one since I am waiting to pick the kids up from their practices. Only one, ok?" Dee heads towards the couch, as Des goes to grabs two beers, and throws his empty bottle in the recycle bin.

Coming around the center island, he watches her as she looks around. Dee looks up at him as he approaches and tells him that his house still looks like a bachelor pad. Then says that he will probably never going to change. He sees she is smiling widely so he just shakes his head and says quietly, "Baby, it needs a woman's touch. You volunteering?"

Dee takes in a sharp breath because it seems that Des is flirting with her, but he hasn't done that since the first time she walked into the shop, and certainly not since their fling ended. She feels her heart beating faster, but says nothing.

With her hands on her lap, Dee looks down so Des doesn't see her blushing face. She doesn't know he is there until she feels him sit down right next to her on the couch. The heat coming off his body is so intense that she can feel his brute power closing in. He leans over and softly breathes in her ear, "no reply, Sugar?"

Lifting her head and looking directly into his unusually sexy, silver eyes, she tells him smugly, "No, I am not volunteering, Boss!!"

28

Shaking his head while running his hands through his hair Des tries to think of what to say next. Dee grabs her beer and takes a long swig of it before placing it on a coaster sitting at the edge of his cocktail table. "Are you going to sign these papers so I can start early in the morning on the work orders?" Reaching for the pile of papers, he precedes to sign wherever there is an X. When he finishes, he pushes them in her direction, and asks, "Happy now?" Dee just nods.

Sitting in silence, the tension between them becomes extremely uncomfortable. Des has no idea why or where the tensions is coming from, but he doesn't like it. They've always had a relaxing relationship even in their teens when they would experiment with their sexuality. Watching Dee from the corner of his eye, she appears skittish and flustered. She's blushing and doing her best to not look in his direction.

Reaching his hand over, he grasps her chin, and turns her to him. "What's going on Dee? You seem really uneasy, so talk to me, sugar." Turning her body towards him, she softly pushes his hand down and pulls away from his touch.

"Nothing is wrong. It's just been a while since I have been in your home. That's all. Funny how it all seems to look like everything is exactly the same. Feels like we are back five or six years ago when I first started working at the shop. Or should I say when we spent a lot of time together outside of the shop. Remember?

He looks around his family room and into the kitchen realizing she is right, he hasn't changed anything since she was here last.

A light bulb instantly goes off in his head. Dee helped him pick out the furniture they are sitting on. She was also involved in picking the appliances for his kitchen. He had been remodeling when they'd had their brief fling when she'd first started at the shop. Since they spent time here, he wanted it to be comfortable for her. It also gave her something to keep her busy. Helping him furnish his home allowed her the time she needed so that the shit with her ex faded slowly out of her mind. So, after the remodeling was done he had asked Dee to help him pick out the furnishings for his home.

He could feel her eyes on him, so he glanced her way, and replied, "Why should I change anything? I like it the way it is."

Dee shakes her head softly and asks, "Do you ever think of when we were together or the stuff we did? I know it was a while ago, but sitting here brings back a lot of good memories for me."

Taking his time, he replies, "Dee we work together every day, so, yes, to answer your question, my mind does drift to one of the best times of my life and what we had. But, you didn't want to continue so I have never pursued you, because I wanted to respect your boundaries. I also didn't want to make you uncomfortable. What's going on, honey? Please just talk to me?"

Clearing her throat Dee starts, "I don't know Des. With the kids getting older, my mind has been playing games with me. Reminiscing over my life or lack thereof, I should say. In a couple of years, both Jagger and Daisy won't need me anymore so the thought of being totally alone is starting to wear on my nerves, that's all."

Pulling her close and ignoring her startled gasp, he gathers her in his arms. Des holds her tight, chest to chest, but says nothing. They just hold on to each other for what seems like eternity, but in fact, is only a few minutes. As he feels her relax into his hold, he moves his hands up into her thick hair that smells like vanilla with a slight flowery fragrance. His intention is to just give her some comfort, but his body has other ideas.

Smelling her hair and feeling her breasts press against his chest, while her hands lay on his upper thighs. He can feel her breathing increase and feels his cock hardening. Fuck! This is not what he wanted to happen. Well yes, he wanted this to happen, but he's not sure it should happen. '"Shit, talk about having a hard on at the wrong place and time."

Her fingers, somehow, must have felt his cock swelling, because Dee immediately pulls away from him.

"Maybe I should go Des, it's getting late. Thanks for signing the papers."

"Sugar, please don't run, maybe we need to talk

some more."

Just as she starts to answer him, her phone starts to ring in her purse. Dee reaches for her cell phone, and Des stands and walks back behind the island, adjusting his cock.

Listening to Dee talk to one of her kids, Des continues to take deep breaths, in order to calm his over excited libido. Ending the call Dee stands up, grabs her beer, and walks over to the kitchen sink. She pours out the remaining beer, and then rinses out the bottle, placing it on the counter.

"Thanks for the beer Des, got to go get my kids. See you in the morning." As she walks by him, he grabs her upper arms, pulling her back to his front. She stands perfectly still, breathing rapidly.

"We need to talk Dee, not tonight, but soon."

She shakes her head as he wraps his arms around her. She feels his arousal pressing between the cheeks of her ass. God it feels so hot and hard. Dee lets out a moan as his hands move up and down her belly. Then she puts her hands on his in order to get him to release her.

Des turns her around, chest to chest. Dee feels his erection on her belly as he lifts her head, while gently holding her cheeks. She watches as he lowers his head and lightly touches his lips to hers for just a moment. Then he moves back just a bit, while watching her closely.

Suddenly, Dee feels like she needs to 'live in the moment', so she reaches up, grasps his hair, to pull him back down, and smashes their lips together.

Immediately, Des regains control of her mouth. His lips are soft but firm at the same time. His tongue glides over her closed lips, and puts pressure on them until she grants him permission to enter. When he nibbles on her fuller, bottom lip, she gasps, and inadvertently grants him entry. He takes advantage of it and he deepens the kiss. They are suddenly both starving for one another and their kiss is like someone had granted them permission to feast. Finally, their most intimate wishes and their desperate longings for each other are being met.

Dee has never felt this way with any other man.

The feeling of being taken care of while the intense heat between them threatens to overwhelm her is amazing. Although she loves being in his arms, Dee pushes on his chest and steps back before their passion gets too out of hand. Both of them are panting and gazing at each other.

Dee grabs her purse along with the papers she brought for him to sign and head off towards the door, honestly not knowing what to say.

Des walks past her and opens the front door for her saying, "Be careful driving sugar, I will see you in the morning. And Dee Dee? We are finally going to have that talk, no way out of it after what we just experienced. Don't fight me on this sweetie, cause ya know you will lose."

Dee steps into her car with the realization that she is in trouble. Des could have any woman he wanted. He always has, as they elegantly—well, sometimes not so elegantly—throw themselves at him. She also knows that over the past several years, he has had multiple lovers in his life. Each affair he'd had ultimately tore a piece from her heart, but she'd had to make a choice for her family.

She knows this because women talk and they all want a chance at Desmond Connelly. Between his gorgeous looks, sense of humor, and just being a great guy, Dee knows woman have been falling at his feet for years.

Dee doesn't understand why he has never been in a relationship. She knows he has been involved with some women, because they also talk. Dee has tried extremely hard to ignore these conversations, because her little green demon comes and listens to what these women have to say about Des. Even after all of these years, she is still pissed that these nameless women get a part of Des that she has never had, but has wanted so badly, it hurts.

Chapter 3—Wolf

After Dee leaves Des grabs another beer trying to clear his head over the two women, he's had interactions with tonight. He remembers Wolf telling him that Katie was a bitch and would cause him nothing but trouble. As usual, Des wonders why he didn't listen to his friend and longtime employee. If he had, maybe that would have saved him some of the headache. Wolf always seems to have a sixth sense when it comes to women and whether or not they were keepers or bitches. Des chuckled at this thought.

Wolf Youngblood was the first employee Des had hired when he'd become the owner of Connelly's. Wolf had been a young man searching for something and had been in a bad way. Des still doesn't even know if Wolf is his real name, but he met him in a bar about ten years ago, when Wolf had been eighteen. Yeah, he had been underage in a bar trying to take on the world. Because of his stature, no one would have questioned the Native American about his age.

Wolf had been sitting at the bar, nursing a beer, and glaring at everyone coming and going. Des had approached him, because his curiosity got the best of him. He knew the kid was underage and was drinking alone. Wolf looked like the perfect example of what a warrior from days gone by might have looked liked. He has long, black hair that reached his waist and wears, at all times, in a braid. He has weathered, honey-colored skin, due to his Indian heritage, with high cheekbones and a sculpted face. His cinnamon brown eyes, at first glance, are emotionless until you have gotten to know him. Most people never take the time to get past the demons in Wolf's eyes. Des has tried for years to help Wolf put his past behind him, but Wolf rarely allows anyone in or speaks of his past. The little knowledge Des knows is that Wolf is Lakota Sioux. He is from out West, and knows that he never speaks about his family outside of his brother.

Besides that, he knows the 'complete package of Wolf' tends to attract women. Des has had first-hand viewing of this in his shop and whenever they go out. Wolf has a way about him that has all women, regardless of age, doing their best to get his attention.

Wolf has never spoken about his 'conquests' in all the years they have known each other. But, Des knows there have been many that have known Wolf intimately although none have ever come to the shop or have bothered Wolf after their time together. Des sees the reaction of females when they go out. Women hungrily watch Wolf all the time, as if they want to eat him alive. The sexual tension that women give off is sometimes overwhelming, but Des never sees Wolf respond to them.

Des knows by the proof of the scars that run up and down his back that Wolf was somehow abused or mistreated. The first time Des saw the monstrosity and cruelty on Wolf's back, he was immediately taken aback and appalled. He tried to talk to him about it, but Wolf's protection shield came up immediately. Over the years, Wolf has tried to hide those scars with tattoos, but even the ink can't hide the horror he has been forced to live through.

Des and time have helped Wolf come to terms with his ability to allow people to get close. Des has seen Wolf open up to some of his co-workers over the years, while others he never gave the time of day and would ignore having nothing to do with them. One person specifically is Katie. She actually went after Wolf first, but he wanted nothing to do with her. Des should have followed suit. Wolf tends to know whom to pick and allow into his simple life.

Wolf is, for the most part, a quiet man. Des has rarely seen Wolf lose his temper a couple of times, but that was enough for Des to know that whatever happened in Wolf's past has not been dealt with. One time it took five guys to pull Wolf off a guy who had been mistreating his girlfriend. Wolf didn't just kick his ass, he took the girl to the hospital, helped her get settled in her own place, and then assisted her to find a job. He continues to check in on Ginger from time to time since they are now close friends. Des remembers another time when a man was beating his dog in the middle of the street with a huge stick. Wolf stormed over grabbed the man by the neck and literally lifted him off his feet, letting him dangle in the air. Wolf then threw the man across the street, and then gently looked after the dog that was in bad shape. After many days at the vet and constant care, the dog managed to survive, and now lives, content, on Wolf's property, Spirit's forever home.

There are many strays that have come and gone from Wolf's ranch and not all of them have been animals. He has the ability to draw all kinds of strays, everything from abused women, broken men or soldiers, runaways, to kids in trouble. He never turns anyone away, always trying to help get them on their feet and toward the road to living a decent life.

Wolf's skill as a fabricator of custom bikes gives him the ability to listen to what a customer describes as their dream bike, and then completes the task to perfection. This still amazes Des. The custom fabrication part of the business continues to grow in leaps and bounds, so Des is considering asking Wolf to go into a partnership with him on the custom bike side of the business. Between the rich son of bitches and the 1% clubs who are calling in orders almost daily, Des is starting to fall behind. He doesn't want to lose the reputation his business has built over the last thirteen years as being one of the best.

Des has also been worried about Wolf for a while. Wolf has been hiding something from Des and it scares him. Some of Wolf's contacts are kinda sketchy and Des doesn't want Wolf pulled into something illegal. Des knows that Wolf's brother lives on the edge and only texts or calls him when he is in some kind of trouble. Wolf has mentioned that he has been in contact with Axe recently. Des is concerned because Axe is part of a 1% MC and doesn't want any trouble. With Axe hanging around, trouble would always be right around the corner. Des needs to have a talk with Wolf ASAP in order to find out the truth of what is going on. The shop has too much to lose if Axe starts trouble and Des doesn't want to see Wolf get hurt. Des is worried about his business, but also concerned about all of the employees that have come to depend on him for their livelihood.

Chapter 4—The Murphys

Des gets up and grabs another beer. He moves back to his desk, reflecting on the rest of his crew at the shop.

Gabriel 'Doc' Murphy came along next. Des knew Doc was an exceptional guy when he saw how he took such phenomenal care of his ill wife, Fern. He hired Doc on the spot because the clinic Doc and Fern opened for the underprivileged lost funding and was closed. The idea of closing the clinic tore the Murphy's apart, emotionally and financially. They believed that the care they were providing, for the community, was beneficial for all. And with the closing of the clinic both Doc and Fern lost their financial stability.

Then Fern became ill. After months of testing, including many misdiagnoses, the doctors discovered that Fern, the love of his life had cancer. Unfortunately, because neither Doc nor Fern had permanent employment, which in turn meant they had no health insurance, so the surmounting bills sent them into a financial downfall. So, when Doc approached Des explaining that he needed to have both permanent employment and insurance, but mostly insurance to help Fern with her cancer, Des hired him on the spot.

Over the years Des had seen how the clinic grew, how Doc and Fern helped so many people in their small town in Indiana that he couldn't turn away Doc. Although Doc had limited mechanical experience, Des knew that he would do his best, not just for Des, but for the shop as well.

Doc turned out to be an exceptional mechanic for someone who had never actually worked on vehicles of any kind. He took to working on motorcycles, especially building choppers, and the specialty bikes. He loves to work on them alone. He has actually helped build that part of the business up with Wolf since there are no other shops close that do specialty builds. Doc is building a name for himself. Because Fern has been so sick, in and out of the hospital, Doc does everything alone.

He is a man struggling with his heart breaking over her illness. Fern is Doc's high school sweetheart, but they have been together since they were fourteen. They graduated high school at the same time and both went away to college together.

When Doc ran out of money for college, he joined the army for a while and that is where he found his love for helping people. He was stationed around the world in third world countries and he learned to make the most of what was provided. Doc showed underprivileged people how to work, in their own countries, with what they had and was trained in the army to be a medic.

When he came home, Doc courted then married Fern, and they worked together to open their clinic. Fern's a registered nurse and Doc had his experiences as a medic from his time in the army. Doctors and nurses volunteered their time at the clinic because, they also wanted to help the Murphy's help the citizens of their community.

When the Murphy's lost the clinic's funding and then the diagnosis regarding Fern's cancer, stress of life increased exponentially. Now, with Fern in the hospital, Doc rarely goes home anymore, unless she comes home for a brief time. He is usually at the shop, working, or at the hospital spending time with Fern. Doc admits that it is difficult to be at home without Fern; too many memories threaten to choke the life from his own body.

Even with health insurance from the shop the bills for Fern's care continue to pile up. Doc confided in Des one night over burgers and beers that he might be forced to sell their house. Des doesn't want that to happen, so he has designed a plan to help the Murphy's, financially. That is if all goes according to Des plans.

☒ ☒ ☒ ☒

Stress and heartbreak have left Doc lonely and more than a tad bit lost. Fern asked Des to find a woman that could help Doc ease his pain and allow him some sexual release. A woman who is not looking for a long-term relationship, just some 'fun'. Someone that could sexually fill in for her during her treatments. She told Des that she felt like she had failed Doc as a wife, lover and a partner.

Fern's desire to make sure her husband was well cared for impressed and amazed Des. He could only imagine how hard her request to him had been. Des knew that there were not a lot of women like Fern; a wife that wanted to give her husband something she thought he needed.

Des didn't even have to try to find a woman for Doc. Doc had more admirers than Des could have ever hoped to find him. But, come to find out, Doc just wasn't interested in anyone other than Fern. It didn't seem to matter where Doc went, there were always women fawning over him; from the shop, the grocery store, and even at the hospital while he was visiting his sick wife. There was just something magnetic about Doc. He was like the flame to the moth.

Women often show up at the shop with casseroles, baked goods, and homemade sweets to try and entice Doc and capture his attention, because they know that Fern is ill and cannot handle his sexual needs for him. Between his wavy, auburn hair and his deep, emerald eyes that are constantly now filled with pain and sadness. Doc, unintentionally, grabs the attention of every hot-blooded woman that is within a one hundred mile radius. His Irish heritage is apparent and that draws people in daily.

Before Fern fell ill, everyone loved to be around Doc. With his jovial personality and contagious laugh he also has a sick sense of humor and he was always cracking jokes and being a real prankster. Doc is a bear of a man. He is built like a lumberjack with huge arms, broad chest, and narrow hips. Ladies immediately stop and stare at him even though he never even notices. Female attention from other women is not what Doc truly desires. All he wants and needs is Fern. In order to curb the attention of other women, he has had a sleeve of tattoos tattooed on one arm. They are all dedicated to Fern; including having her name tattooed on his forearm and their wedding date included on his bicep under two intertwined tribal hearts.

With his big heart, Doc continues to try to help out by handling any small injuries or illnesses in the community. He has managed to maintain his license as a medical clinician, as well as obtaining his certification in professional bike building for the shop. Des knows that the constant battle Fern is fighting is taking a toll on Doc, so he has a plan to assist the Murphy's with all the medical bills that are piling up. Even with the shop's insurance, it is overwhelming for them. Des will need everyone's help to make his plan work, because it could make the Murphy's bills disappear.

Chapter 5—Memories

Des gets up, throws his bottle away and opens the fridge. Not much in there, but he sees a frozen pizza, so he turns the oven on to heat up. He goes into his bedroom, cleaning up from the tryst with Katie. The room smells of sex, perfume, and sweat. He opens a window, pulls the sheet off the bed, and replaces it with a clean one. Looking around his room, he finds Katie's bra hanging on a chair in his room.

He picks it up; wondering why the arrangement they'd had become so fucked up. He'd thought it worked for both of them, but obviously Katie wanted more and there wasn't any way he was going there. Especially not with her because everyone knew she was as easy as the day was long. He was never disillusioned that they had something special going on. Des had always taken it for what it was.., sex. Occasionally, he would go as far as to get her a little something special, like some new perfume or a piece of jewelry, so she didn't, at least, feel like a whore. Des never treated women, even easy women, like they were worthless. He was open minded and believed that a woman could have the same opportunity that men do to only have sexual relationships without strings attached.

Katie's jealous mind got pissed about Dee Dee. Damn! Des felt his cock start to harden just thinking of her name. What the fuck? Why can't anything ever work out to his advantage or satisfaction? Now he is sitting alone, at home with a boner, a beer in his hand, and Dee on his mind. Come to think of it whenever he had Dee in his thoughts he usually always had a boner. Go figure.

Des puts his beer down, reaches for the buttons on his jeans in order to release his dick. His cock is as hard as steel as he continues to see Dee in his mind; how she looked and felt in his arms. The pre-cum is leaking out the slit on top of his long length, so he uses it to give him some lubrication as he starts to move his hand up and then down. Damn, he wished it was Dee Dee's hand jerking him off.

Even thinking about that makes him harder and hornier. Des' breathing increases as he puts more pressure on his cock, moving his hand faster and faster.

He feels the pressure start in his balls, while his thigh muscles tighten as he continues the onslaught of pressure and the quick up and down motion. Knowing that he is not going to last long, he pulls his shirt up just as long streams of creamy cum land on his flat, muscular stomach. Even though this was the second time his cock had released, he was once again left with an empty feeling. He is reminded that he is without anyone, especially Dee, and his softening cock in his own hand. So much for taking care of his boner, he thinks with a smirk.

Speaking of boners, Cadence comes to mind immediately, and Des smiles. The kid is definitely a man-whore and doesn't hide it. That doesn't keep the women off him, nor does it keep the trouble from his door either.

Chapter 6—Cadence

Des remembers, with a shudder, how Cadence came to be part of Wheels & Hogs a couple of years ago. Not a good memory at all for him.

Cadence Power showed up on the property of Wheels and Hogs half dead. Des was cleaning out a section of woods behind the shop, heard some noises, and some muffled moaning. As he approached, he thought Cadence was dying or close to dead due to the large amount of blood around him. What was left of his clothes barely covered him and from what Des could see it had been more than a beating that left him there. The kid had been tortured, abused, and also looked to have been raped. All he knew was if he didn't step in and try to help the stranger, he was going to die on his property. Des didn't know if someone dropped him off, because the shop was on the outskirts of town or if Cadence had managed to drag himself there.

As soon as Des found him, he called Doc to help get him in the shop's empty apartment upstairs. It took weeks for Cadence to start functioning again. For the first couple of days, it was touch and go because no one knew if he would make it. Doc and Fern had played a large part in helping him heal. Cadence was leery at first, and he didn't trust anyone. Fern was able to put him at ease and eventually gained his trust. She worked with him not only on the physical, but the emotional trauma he had experienced. The kid had fractured bones and cuts that required stitches, as did his head, which was split open. Fern and Doc handled those. Some of his piercings had been yanked out, so Doc helped repair those.

When Cadence started the healing process, he became withdrawn and moody. No one knew what was going on, but eventually, Doc and Fern figured out he was having an issue with some of his injuries that were not going to heal without additional medical assistance. With professional help, Cadence finally explained what was bothering him and Doc decided to take to him to see a specialist. Cadence had to have surgery to repair the damage and tearing that had occurred when whatever had happened to him took place, be it a rape or violation.

Des never asked the kid, he figured if Cadence wanted him to know, he would tell him. Des figured whatever had happened must have been pretty bad, because Cadence had never spoken to him about how he had come to land half beaten to death at the back of Des' property. Des knew that Fern has gotten some of the information from Cadence regarding the incident. Sometimes he watched Fern looking at Cadence with such pain in her eyes that Des had been tempted to ask, but to this day has never broached the subject. The relationship between Fern and Cadence is something to watch though. Fern had taken on the role of mother and protector to him. Now that Fern is sick, it is Cadence that's with Doc for Fern. Des sees the torture in Cadence when anyone talks about Fern and her cancer. The kid wants to save her like she saved him.

Des knows that the kid is from somewhere in the Midwest, and has family, but he doesn't talk to any of them. Des knows he has two brothers and a mother. But in all the time the kid has been at the shop, he has never received a phone call or a piece of mail from any family that Des is aware of. Every holiday he is either with Fern and Doc or some bitch he's picked up. And Cadence can charm the pants off of men, women, and children. Everyone who comes in contact with him, loves his goofy personality.

This kid, for some reason, has burrowed into Des's heart. Cadence fought to recover from his injuries, he never complained once, and he even went so far as to tell Des he would pay him back for everything. Once Cadence was physically able to, he started working in the shop. Even when he was charming his next conquest, Des saw a loneliness in his eyes that made Des realize how truly alone Cadence was and how he held his true self from people, in order to save his heart from breaking again by getting too emotionally attached.

That would be everyone but Fern. She has the ability to affect everyone with her gentle and motherly ways. Over the years Des knows that Cadence would seek out Fern for advice here and there with what was going on in his life.

Des has come to the conclusion that Cadence is a womanizer and man-whore. He never discriminates due to age, size, color, or anything. He just loved women in general.

Des had seen Cadence go for anything that actually had a set of tits and a pussy, no joke. Cadence will find a young, good-looking thing to fuck for a night or two; while she looked at him like he was the cat's meow. They always seemed to hope he would keep them around for a while. The next woman Cadence would show up with would be a slightly overweight, middle-aged woman who looked like she knew how lucky she was to be with him. They never lasted long, just enough time for him to get his rocks off. No commitment, dating, or involvement... ever.

Cadence just loves women. And they love him back. He stands around 6'0" and is every woman's dream guy. Thick wheat colored hair, just a bit on the long side. And he is built like a Greek God with ripped muscles throughout his body.

But what women love most about Cadence, and Des has heard this time and time again, are his eyes. Cadence has eyes so dark they look almost black. You can't make out his eye color from his pupils until you get really close and see the midnight blue ring around them. His eyes drive women crazy. But, so does everything else he does, from his easy going personality to the tattoos, and from the piercings he has all over his body to the deep timbre of his voice.

The kid can karaoke with the best of them and dance like he just came off of a reality TV show. That's just how good he is. All of his talents bring women from near and far; each new woman thinks she is going to be the one, until Cadence kicks her to the curb. Des should know, as he's usually the one picking up the pieces after one of Cadence's indiscretions falls apart, escorting them from his shop, the parking lot, or wherever Cadence tends to leave them. The kid has a lot to learn, but he is a good kid who works hard and never complains to Des regarding whatever he's had to do in the shop.

His skills on cars, including being able to diagnosis what is wrong with an automobile, is truly amazing to Des. The kid has never been formally trained and is better than anyone Des has ever worked with.

Des hopes with everything going on, that Cadence

will step up and help with all the changes that are coming in the near future, especially with his plans for Doc and Fern and their mounting hospital expenses. He knows that if any of this is going to work, he will need all of his crew to be on board.

Just as the timer goes off for his frozen pizza, Des hears the front door bell rings and he wonders who that might be. He lives outside of town and his house is out of the way of normal traffic. Des turns the timer off as someone pushes the bell again. "Fuck, no patience," Des screams. "I coming, give me a goddamn second," he says as he loses his patience. "What kind of asshole rides a door bell?"

As he reaches the door and swings it open, he sees Katie with her finger on the bell. "What the fuck Katie, now what?" She lifts her hand with a bag of take-out food in it. "Are ya hungry Des?" He just shakes his head and lets her follow him down the hallway to the kitchen as he goes to pull the pizza out of the oven.

He feels her coming up behind him and she wraps her arms around his waist putting her hand on his six-pack. Des takes a deep breath telling her softly, "Katie, we are done, honey, come on, don't make it any harder than it has to be. We have already talked about this, there is no going back, darling. Our time for fun ended hours ago and I don't personally plan on continuing it any longer."

She giggles, her hand moves to his crotch, and she tells him, "We need to make it harder." And then she squeezes his half hard dick. Des tries to pull her hands up and away from his crotch, but she starts moving her hand up and down on his cock and he feels it start to harden. Damn, why can't he control his own fucking cock? He can feel her confidence building as he roughly pulls away.

He looks at her and says rudely, "The food is gonna get fuckin cold. Now, you want to eat or you can go, either way no skin off my ass." He knows he is being a jerk, or better yet an asshole, but she is just making this harder for both of them. Their sexual relationship was now over and since they weren't friends, he didn't want there to be any miscommunications with her on their lack of a relationship subject. He also doesn't want her. Des doesn't want to lead her on or mess with her emotions. He wasn't looking for a relationship with her, he just wanted some casual sex, but that was now over.

As she picks up a burger out of the bag, Katie's blue eyes sparkle with her anger and she spits at him, "If I was Dee Dee you wouldn't care if the food got cold or not would you, Des?" He continues to stare her down, but Katie doesn't back down and keeps running her mouth. "What does she got that I don't, huh?" Des considers her question and looks Katie right in the eyes and says, "Class, sweetie. Morals. Values. Shall I go on?"

Katie throws the burger at him as she storms to the counter, grabs the remaining food in the bag, and slams out the front door. He hears her car squeal out of his driveway. He shrugs his shoulders, cleans the burger off the floor and goes to eat his now lukewarm pizza.

Chapter 7—Dee Dee

While Des eats his pizza, he thinks about Katie's comments about Dee Dee and memories overcome him. He met Dee in high school, noticing her immediately. Her long, honey-brown hair almost touched her ass and she had the most unique amber eyes he had ever seen. Des was taken aback by her, but didn't know how to approach her. They'd had some classes together so eventually they met. When he got to know her he realized that she was funny and goofy, and it made him want to spend more time with her. During the next couple of years, Des and Dee Dee, formed a solid friendship that grew stronger, and one where they were always there if the other needed someone to talk to, or a shoulder to cry on.

Over the years, there had been some intimate moments between them. It had started out as teenagers hooking up here and there. He remembered the first time they'd kissed at a party; they had both been a bit intoxicated. Dee Dee's lips had been so fucking soft, and he could tell that she hadn't had a lot of experience by the way she kissed him back.

They never dated, but seemed to be in the same place at the same time a lot. He even took her to a dance her sophomore year, because no one had asked her, and Dee was devastated. She looked beautiful in her burnt orange dress. He lost his mind when he first saw her coming down the stairs at her house. Never having learned to dance, she taught him that night. Being able to hold a developing Dee in his arms had made him so horny the entire evening. When the dance ended, they went down by the lake, sat in his beat up truck, and made out. She seemed to have a bit more experience than she had with their first kiss. They were all over each other like dogs in heat. He finger fucked her that night in his truck, loving the sounds coming out of her mouth. The way she would say his full name 'Desmond' was unbelievable. She only rubbed over his hard cock through his pants. He would never pressure her, so Dee jerked him off, and he came in his dress slacks, but it was probably one of the best experiences he'd ever had in his entire life. Time went on, they both entered and ended relationships with others, but they always seemed to connect here and there.

When his family's tragedy took place, and then later, his business venture including building the shop's reputation and clientele, he didn't see Dee Dee often. He'd heard she'd gotten married, and had some kids.

Then out of the blue Dee Dee answered the ad he had posted for his office manager. If Des had thought she was something in high school, he would have been wrong, because now, she was a total knockout. She was a curvy woman just the way he liked; she stood around 5'6" and had a shape on her that caught every guy's eye. Dee Dee had an hourglass figure with a rack that drew his eyes all the time, a small waist, and hips with an ass that made his mouth water daily. Her legs were nice and firm and made her look taller than she was.

She had been in a brutal situation that had needed to come to an end. Dee needed a job with some form of income before she left the asshole she was living with. Turns out when Dee Dee took the job in the shop, her ex thought that meant a meal ticket. Des knew things weren't healthy or safe, when she showed up to work one day with black and blue bruise marks all up and down both arms. She sported a busted lip, a black eye, had been holding her two small children's hands, and asked Des for help. It was then that he realized how bad it actually was.

Des gathered up some of the guys from the shop to pay a cordial visit to the asshole. Dee never heard from him again. Des helped her into a house in town that had enough room for her and the kids. Time and less stress seemed to help Dee heal from her abusive relationship.

So, in return for his help, Dee kept the shop running efficient and she mothered all the guys in the shop. She never played favorites with any of the boys.

Between running the shop and raising her two kids, Dee stays busy. Her kids now work around the shop, on weekends and during summer break, for extra cash. Des likes both Jagger and Daisy, probably because they are from their momma.

They're exceptional kids that work hard, and never seemed to give their mother a hard time, which for teenagers, was almost a miracle.

Jagger's a fifteen year old, long-limbed boy trying

to grow into his body. He's quiet, even tempered, works hard, and never causes any trouble. Jagger seemed to like watching, both Wolf and Doc, build the bikes. In the last year, he had been helping with small repairs on the bikes. Jagger is saving all his money, because he wants to either build his own bike or buy one of the older ones in the shop. Dee is not too happy about that, but hasn't told Jagger no yet.

Daisy is thirteen and a total knockout like her mother. She is a smart ass with attitude who loves to push everyone's buttons. On more than one occasion, Dee has had to step in to rescue her young daughter from her smart mouth. Daisy has a crush on Cadence, and has been following him around like a little puppy for years. Dee has already had a talk with Cadence, warning him that if he ever touches or hurts her daughter no one would ever find his body parts. For once, Des saw Cadence actually have some real fear in his eyes. Cadence watches out for Daisy like he would a kid sister which Daisy is not fond of. She doesn't think of Cadence as a brother since he is her first teenage crush.

On the whole, Dee Dee's household is perfect. Des would love to pursue Dee, but as far as he knows she tends not to date at all. And, if it didn't work out again, he would feel like shit, because it would affect the kids. Des, against better judgment, has come to care a tremendous deal for Jagger and Daisy. Not to mention how that would affect the dichotomy of the shop while he is the owner and Dee working as the office manager. If the relationship didn't work out, it could mess with his shop.

The guys all assumed he wanted Dee for himself. They don't know that after Dee left her asshole ex that for a while they'd a sexual relationship. It didn't happen overnight because she'd had to heal from the ex's abuse in her body, her spirit and most important in her head, but it had happened.

Their connection was intense, hot, sensual and rewarding. But, for some reason they'd never taken it all the way to actual intercourse just oral, hand jobs, or finger fucking. They would spend time together, either at the shop or his house. *Remembering how she would blow him, instantly makes his cock start to harden.* But, as her children grew older, Dee didn't want to give them the wrong impression. So, she'd explained this to Des, and, together, they had decided it was best to end that part of their relationship.

Still, to this day, the sexual tension is there, and he can feel her eyes on him when they are in the shop together, but he has not stepped over that line again. That was what Katie was for, the occasional sexual encounter with no commitment. But, that didn't work out like he thought it would as tonight revealed. He is getting too old to sit around and wait for the perfect time to become involved with Dee again while fucking all the easy women, around town and surrounding areas.

The time might finally be right to see if he and Dee Dee have anything besides just the obvious chemistry and undeniable friendship. Des thinks, 'just maybe' because of her most welcome, but unscheduled visit tonight.

Chapter 8—Willow & Archie

Time went by and Des's business grew at the shop, so he hired two part timers to help out Dee. Willow and Archie. Both girls were in their mid-twenties and couldn't be more different.

Willow's name fit her to a tee. She's tall 5'9", thin but curvy, simply stunning with long mahogany hair, and bright sky blue eyes. Willow is extremely shy and quiet, too. She helps with the books, fills orders with Dee, and books appointments. Willow is a wiz with the electronics and has helped Dee Dee update all of the phone and computer systems in the shop. She is always educating Des and the guys on the newest advances in technology out there. Everyone that meets Willow, seem to love her the instant they connect.

Willow loves to work outside with flowers, so she is now in charge of all the landscaping and flower boxes around Des's shop. Over the last year or so, Willow's, single handling, changed the appearance of the exterior of the shop. Willow even got both of Dee's kids involved; Daisy, with Willow's help, maintained the flowers and Jagger was instructed to maintain the lawn.

Willow is fascinated with Wolf, and if she is not working with Dee or in her flower-beds, she is keeping a close eye on him. Des worries about the situation because Wolf seems clueless. Willow has a crush, a hero worship or some kind of fascination with him. Des doesn't want Willow to get hurt, but he wants to give it some time to see where it leads. Already, he has watched Willow fall apart or worse draw into herself as one or more women flirted with Wolf, a couple of different times. Even though Wolf has not shown any interest towards Willow, Des can see her heart's gentle feelings written all over her face. Since she started working at the shop, Willow has never dated as far as Des knew. It is more than likely, she is waiting for Wolf to wake up and notice her.

Archie is loud, obnoxious, and a serious tomboy. She has shoulder-length, auburn-colored hair and hazel eyes.

She has multiple piercings and is now starting to

get tattoos. Archie already has half of a sleeve done on one arm in brilliant colors.

Archie takes no shit from anyone and is always punching and pinching the guys when they tease her. She hides behind her tough exterior, but Des knows that she is hiding something more. There are times when she doesn't think anyone is watching, she lets her guard down, and looks like an inexperienced young girl who is troubled and confused.

Archie can hold her own next to any of his guys when it comes to working on cars or bikes. She never told them how she came to know so much in regards to the mechanics side of the business, but she is in fact exceptional at what she does. There's been many times when she's stepped in to help when he needed it. If they were behind or one of the guys called off sick, he knew he could count on her. Des has begun to let Archie handle all the small jobs including oil changes, tire rotation, tune ups, etc. Archie seems to feel more at home in the shop than in the office with Dee & Willow.

Des keeps a close watch on both Willow and Archie

because neither have family in town. They share an apartment together that Des made sure it was not just functional, but safe before they moved in. He has regular visits to not only check in on them, but also to fix things for them when needed.

Sometimes he feels like their dad when they have an issue or concern because they always come to him first for his advice, because they both trust what he tells them.

Des begins to relax and he comes to the realization that he has built his own tight knit group, or family in other words, inside his shop over the past few years.

All of them have come to mean so much to him. Even though he doesn't on the surface show his emotions, he would do anything to help, nurture, and protect each and every one of them.

As the night seems to fly by, he finishes his pizza, cleans up the kitchen, and is relaxing and watching some shit on TV when his mind grabs hold of a couple of things.

First, he still has Katie's bra, which he will need to return, and it sucks, too. Because that means, he will be forced to have at least one more interaction with her after this extremely fucked up night. He didn't have a positive feeling about seeing her again so soon after ending their arrangement. Katie doesn't seem to be the type of woman who can be mature in situations like this.

Second, he needs to have a meeting with his employees to inform them of his upcoming plans. Des knows that he is going to need everyone on board, because there are some major changes that are coming to their sleepy, little town. For some of his employees, it's just going to be more work, but for others, it may very well turn out to be a life or death situation.

His last thought, Des decides it is time to shit or get off the pot. He is going to pursue Dee Dee in a real relationship. The thought scares the shit out of him, but he wants it all, including her kids and maybe even some kids of their own. He just has to be careful, so he doesn't scare her off and screw this up with his insecurities about relationships in general.

Later that evening as he lay in bed, Des thought about what was coming next and all of the excitement that the changes would bring. He set his alarm for the next morning and turned on his iPod. Since he was a kid, he'd always needed music on so he could fall asleep. When he closes his eyes, the first verse of, "Bless the Broken Road," begins to play. The words seem to come straight from his heart. They speak of going down a narrow way and finding a true love along that broken road. Des feels like the words are his words about his life.

As his mind started to shut down, and he drifted towards sleep, Des realized how true this song reflected his life. Deep down he wanted, no needed to find that one person that completed him. And shit, he had gotten lost a time or twenty. But, he had come to realize where the road had been leading him to, time again. Dee Dee was always at the end of his road. He just needed to get there in one piece.

Chapter 9—The Future

With the beginning of a new day with the sun starting to rise, Des is woken from a deep sleep by the light filtering through his blinds. Stretching his arms above his head, he runs his hands through his hair and climbs out of bed. Des is hoping that today is a better day than yesterday; with all the drama, and then his reflections of his crew at Wheels and Hogs. Going down memory lane, remembering how they all came to him made Des realize how truly blessed he is, having all of them in his life.

After taking care of business in the bathroom, running some water over his face, and brushing his teeth, Des heads to the kitchen. He can still smell the pizza he ate for dinner the previous evening. He starts the coffee and heads to his office. He has a lot of work to do in order to get his plan in place. After sitting at his desk he thinks about the enormous task he has taken on, but he knows Doc and Fern are worth it.

After Des spoke to Doc, two weeks ago, he knew something had to be done. The tests Fern had undergone showed that her cancer had not gone into remission, but had continued to grow. That meant the treatment course they were currently on wasn't working. The next step would be to go to a stronger treatment and that meant a bone marrow transplant. The thought shook Des to his core, because if they couldn't find a donor or it didn't work, it meant they would lose Fern. That is not an option he is willing to accept.

Des headed back to the kitchen, poured himself a cup of Jo and added some cream from the fridge. Looking out his window to the deck he sees two squirrels playing around the furniture. The sight brings a smile to his face; he realizes the simplest things in life can bring a smile to your face and lighten the load in your heart.

Back in his office he opens the file on his desk, and then turns on his computer. He has some research to do so when he presents the plan to his crew they will understand that he had done his due diligence in order to help the Murphys. He wants to show them that the plan isn't just a long shot, but could actually be a cure for their beloved Fern. Looking at his emails, he sees a response email from the Bone Marrow Registry. Opening it, he finds one of the longest emails he has ever received. Setting his coffee down, he begins reading. The contact from the Registry, Sue Thompson had gone into extreme detail to explain how they would be able to assist with the plan Des concocted. According to Sue, the registry was in need of donors so she thought that if Wheels & Hogs did a Charity ride for Fern and included the registry both Fern and the Registry greatly benefit. Fern could get her donor, God willing, and the registry would be able to increase their donor population. Des had no idea about all of the regulations and rules that were involved in the undertaking he had planned, but he was determined.

After reading Sue's email he starts opening the list of attachments she'd forwarded to him. Holy shit, he is going to need an attorney to look over all of these forms. His initial plan was to have the entire donor related information at the end of the charity ride in his small town in Indiana. He figured that would be the easiest way to keep this under control. Sue has other ideas about setting up something similar to kiosks at all the stops so if someone who has signed up for the ride decides they don't want to do the entire ride they can still be tested by the organization.

After printing up all the forms Des continued to go

through his emails. Some of them were junk, but a couple were from some of his brothers in MC clubs confirming that they were on board to help out Doc and Fern. Des starts taking notes on which clubs had responded and how they wanted to get involved with this Charity ride.

There were two main objectives to this ride. To raise money to assist Doc and Fern with all they're outstanding hospital bills and their personal bills including their mortgage. Second to assist the donor registry so maybe they could find a match for Fern.

Des has researched the process to be a donor and depending on how they obtained a sample either by cheek swab or a blood test that gets you on the donor list. If you match an additional blood test will be necessary.

Des starts taking down some notes. There was so much to do and he realized that he could not do this all by himself. He had his MC Brothers already on board from as far as California to his neighbors in Illinois. Writing down each club that responded along with what they either wanted to participate in or donate to the cause. The list continued to grow as he went through the emails on his computer.

Once he completed the MC information, he starts to arrange the emails by importance to the cause. Some emails were in reply from his original requesting donations of any kind. After counting twenty or more he knew the meeting with crew had to happen sooner rather than later. Printing all these emails up; he puts them in a file, which he writes on the tab 'Donations'.

Next he reviews the email from Doc regarding all of their outstanding debt. Des takes a deep breath not realizing how bad it was. Even with the group health plan through Wheels and Hogs a lot of the treatments and medications are either excluded or at a high cost according to Doc. Not to mention if the treatment was experimental and there was a cost, it would generally be financially draining as the group medical didn't cover little or no of experimental procedures and pharmaceutical costs. The final number was staggering to Des. How the hell have Doc and Fern managed knowing they were drowning in debt? This additional pressure was something neither of them needed at this time in their lives. From what Doc has relayed to Des, Fern was getting weaker every day. The new treatment was to start in the next couple of weeks. They were trying to build up her immune system, because it was so beaten from all the prior treatments. 'Fuck, how could this happen to such a nice couple', Des thinks.

Spending a couple of hours outlining his ideas on paper helped him prepare to involve his people. If nothing else Des wanted to be prepared to answer any and all of their questions to the best of his ability. Des goes through his day; his mind starts to realize the enormous project he has taken on for his friends. This could turn out two ways and Des is hoping for the first. It could be the best Charity ride ever; raising enough money to assist the Murphy's with all of their outstanding debt. More importantly they find a donor for Fern so her fight with this cancer can finally be over. Or it can turn out to be a bust and that would let Fern and Doc down. Des was starting to feel the pressure of his undertaking. He was going to need assistance to make this a success. Des was hoping and praying that the crew at Wheels and Hogs had the same inspiration to help their friends as he did. It was time to get off his ass and present this to them. Time was ticking by and they had a deadline to get this Charity Ride done. Weather in Indiana wasn't the most co-operative.

For his business and his employees there were a lot of changes coming to Wheels and Hogs both professionally and personally and Des hoped everyone was ready to take that wild ride with him.

Little does he know that this decision is going to be the beginning of a new chapter regarding both his professional and personal life!

Nothing will ever be the same at Wheels & Hogs. The winds of change are in the air, and time will tell if what is coming will be phenomenal or totally shitty for all involved.

To be continued...

Made in the USA
San Bernardino, CA
01 September 2014